Everett Anderson's Goodbye

Everett Anderson's Goodbye

by Lucille Clifton
illustrated by
Ann Grifalconi

SQUARE
FISH

Henry Holt and Company | New York

SQUARE
FISH

An Imprint of Macmillan

EVERETT ANDERSON'S GOODBYE. Text copyright © 1983 by Lucille Clifton.
Illustrations copyright © 1983 by Ann Grifalconi. All rights reserved.
Printed in Mexico by R. R. Donnelley & Sons Company, Reynosa, Tamaulipas.
For information, address Square Fish, 175 Fifth Avenue, New York, NY 10010.

Square Fish and the Square Fish logo are trademarks of Macmillan and
are used by Henry Holt and Company under license from Macmillan.

Library of Congress Cataloging-in-Publication Data
Clifton, Lucille.
Everett Anderson's goodbye / by Lucille Clifton ; illustrated by Ann Grifalconi.
Summary: Everett Anderson has a difficult time coming to terms with his grief after his father dies.
ISBN 978-0-8050-0800-5
[1. Stories in rhyme. 2. Death—Fiction. 3. Fathers and sons—Fiction.]
I. Grifalconi, Ann, ill. II. Title.
PZ8.3.C573Evh 1983   [E]   82-23426

Originally published in the United States by Henry Holt and Company
First Square Fish Edition: September 2012
Square Fish logo designed by Filomena Tuosto
mackids.com

30 29 28

AR: 2.5 / LEXILE: NP

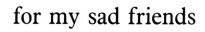
for my sad friends

1 Denial
2 Anger
3 Bargaining
4 Depression
5 Acceptance

The Five Stages of Grief

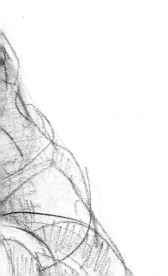

1

Everett Anderson holds the hand
of his mama until he falls asleep
and dreams about Daddy
in his chair, and
at the park, and
everywhere.
Daddy always laughing or never,
just Daddy, Daddy, forever and ever.

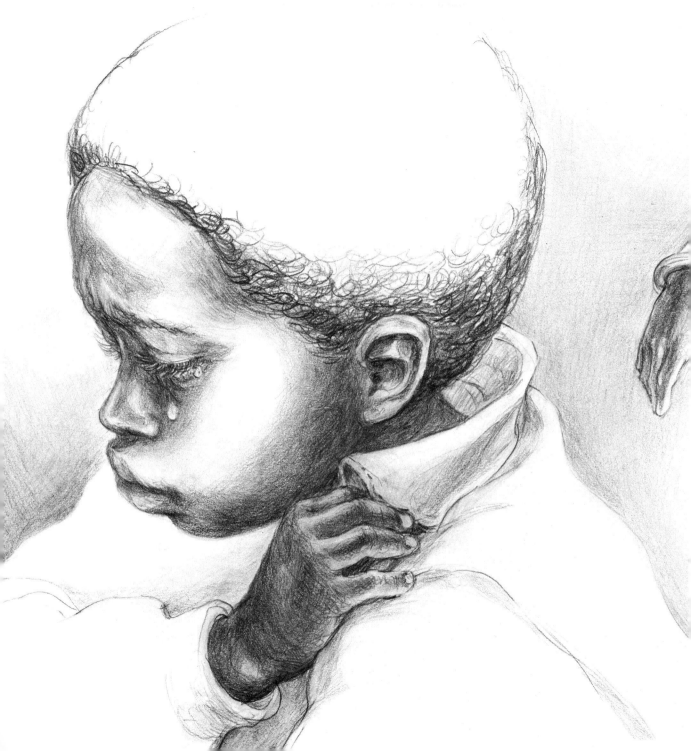

2

"I don't love Baby Evelyn
   and I don't love Mr. Perry, too,
   and I don't love Christmas or
   Santa Claus
   and I don't love candy
   and I don't love you!"

"Well, Everett," his mama sighs,
"who do you love?"

   And he cries and cries.

3

"I promise to learn my
  nine times nine
  and never sleep late or
  gobble my bread
  if I can see Daddy
  walking, and talking, and
  waving his hand, and
  turning his head.

"I will do everything you say
  if Daddy can be alive today."

4

Everett Anderson tries to sleep
but it is too hard and
the hurt is too deep.

Everett Anderson likes his food
but how can a dinner
do any good?

Everett Anderson just sits staring,
wondering what's the use of caring.

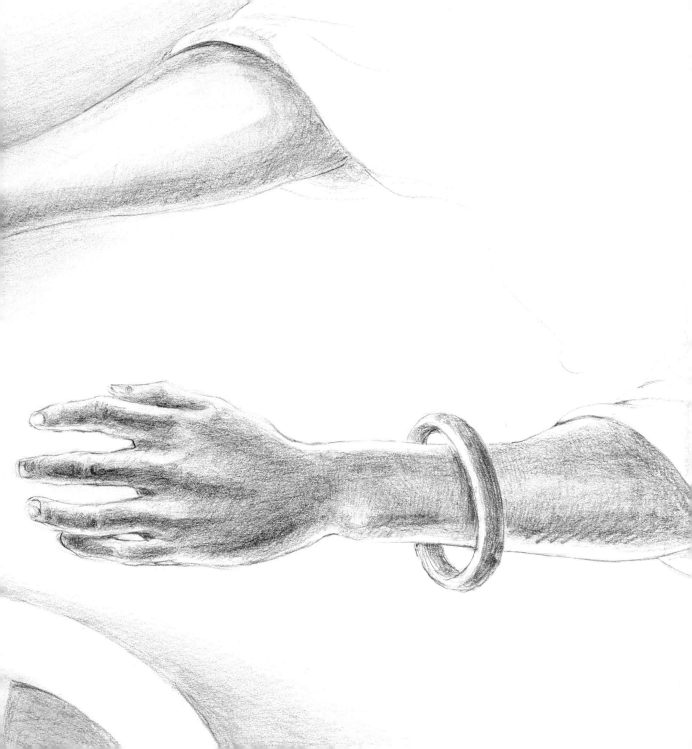

5

After a little bit of time

Everett Anderson says, "I knew
my daddy loved me through and through,
and whatever happens when people die,

love doesn't stop, and
neither will I."